Little Flame and Other Endings

Frank Foley

Copyright © Frank Foley 2016

This paperback edition 2019

Version 2.0

ISBN: 978-1-980-92035-9

For dad, laughing at skinny back prawns, and mum, for the emperor's new clothes. Always that.

Contents

Little Flame 6
Shoelaces 7
Almost a Week 9
That's What August Is 10
Big Chief Antler 11
Why The Hell Would I Do That? 13
Another Week in Rio 14
Softly Sleeps the Calm 17
Trust 19
Love and Catches 1 22
Sometimes You'd Think You Were Goddesses 23
Seventy-Six Trombones 25
The End of Something 26
Joe Theisman's Leg 28
Sunlight on the Side of a House 30
I Should Have Said Something 32
The Mentor 33
Something Not So New 35
Frozen Peas 37
Forget Me, Joe 39
The Juggler 41
Slag Monkey 43
Duration 46
Fountain 47
Tuesday 11th September 2001 49

Love and Catches 2... 50

Little Flame

My new cooker was delivered today, but I had to send it back. I needed a new cooker because the old one had little pictures of flames around the knobs for turning the gas up and down...

Emily was at my house making dinner. She put a pot on the cooker and left the gas way up on big flame. Things would always burn on big flame.

"No, no," I said, "you have to put it on little flame, otherwise it'll burn."

Emily stood there looking at me and I remember the exact shade of her hair and the little pout she had on her lips. Then she was smiling and putting her arms around me. "Little flame," she said. "Oh, you are priceless."

It's difficult to use a cooker that has pictures of little flames and you call them little flames, and you know this makes someone love you because it's innocent and you. In the end I couldn't go near the damn thing. All I could see were the little flames and I could hear Emily saying, "You are priceless," and holding on to me as though we were branded into each other.

When it came the new cooker didn't have pictures of flames. It just had a zero for when the gas is off and a nine for when you want to burn things.

Shoelaces

She said she wanted someone's shoelaces and everyone laughed. It was hot by the pool and everyone was drunk.

She sat on the lounger with a black bikini on. There wasn't much material in that bikini. The thin black bands lisped around her hips and disappeared between her thighs, and every single one of them was catching a sly look.

She said she really needed someone's shoelaces. She looked at me and came over and stood right in front of me. I was sitting on a sun-lounger.

"How the hell can I tie him up without shoelaces?" she said.

Every one of the boys laughed like they couldn't believe this and I sat there cool, smiling, but inside I felt like a king.

She turned around to them. Her long body was tanned and slim. She had strong full hips and slender athletic legs. Her hair was dark from the water, but drying back to its lighter blonde.

Every one of them was looking at her.

"I want to go upstairs," she said. Then she said something else and looked at me and smiled at me and none of the boys could believe what she had said.

"That's what I want to do, and I really want to do it ... so, please, somebody give me some fucking shoelaces."

She said it softly like an innocent girl, like butter wouldn't melt.

I sat there smiling and she was smiling and the boys had these amazed "lucky bastard" looks on their faces. Then Joe started unlacing his Nikes.

"Oh, thank you, Joe," she said and kissed him on the cheek. Then she took my hand and led me up to her room.

Later the boys said she was like the most innocent girl you could meet.

I laughed at that the next day. We were having beers.

Almost a Week

"When will you be home?"

She looked through the dark to the window then closed her eyes. She yawned and tried to sound tired. "Tuesday, maybe Wednesday," she said.

"Almost a week," he said.

"Maybe, yes."

She tried to concentrate on the voices outside in the street. The pubs were turning out again and she could hear people shouting and laughing.

"Is he going?"

She didn't move. For a moment she didn't even breathe. She let the question settle in the air.

"Who?" she said.

She could feel him next to her and he was rigid, not moving. He didn't say a word. The way he was she knew he had his eyes open.

"I don't know," she said. "Probably not."

There was a tiny pause, just a few seconds in the darkness when there was no sound, not even from outside. Then he turned over. He had his back to her now. She could hear him breathing.

She looked over to the window, but it was too dark to see anything clearly.

"Don't be silly," she said.

That's What August Is

Hermione came into the kitchen still wearing that dressing-gown. Her hair was pulled back in a pony-tail and she was singing about Billy Joe Macalister jumping off a bridge.

I tried to block it out. "Hungry?" I said.

"Why would I be hungry?" she said.

Hermione said this in a way that bore right into me. I felt like I was in a microwave, cooking from the inside.

"You should eat something," I said.

Hermione sat gently in a chair. She stared out the window and started to sing about Billy Joe again, strangely upbeat and chipper, like he was a friend of hers and hadn't jumped off a bridge at all.

When I finally did come over and sit down, she smiled at me, an honest awful smile, and covered my hand with hers.

We had the windows open and the August morning was pouring in.

*

I can't explain this to my wife when she asks me about it. When a song comes on the radio on a Sunday morning and she asks me about it, and why I look that way.

That's what August is, I want to say. *That's what August always is.*

But I couldn't even begin to explain.

Big Chief Antler

You can talk, she thought, it's all right for you. It was Sunday again and they were walking in Richmond Park.

"You're not even listening," he said. "You're not even bothering to listen."

"I am listening," she said. In the distance she could see a stag sitting under a tree.

"You have that look on your face where you're miles away."

"I'm listening. I just saw him, Big Chief Antler there."

She pointed into the distance and he stopped walking and a twig snapped under his foot. It sounded like an arm breaking.

"Brilliant," he said, "brilliant. I'm trying to talk to you, and all you can think about is a fucking deer."

She looked up at him under her eyebrows. "It's not a deer, dear," she said. "It's a stag."

*

When she came to the park again, she was on her own. She had the papers tucked under her arm and a flask in her shoulder bag. She walked for half an hour before she found the stag, and sat on the grass a good distance away and poured herself a cup of tea.

She watched him for a long time, just sitting there proud and strong and bored.

Fine, light rain began to fall and she took a hat out of her bag and put it on. She wanted to speak to the stag that was the crux of it. She wanted to march right over there and get it all off her chest, spilling it all to a huge pair of antlers.

The stag just sat there immensely bored, waiting for his time.

*

"So," she said. "That's pretty much the gist of it."

The stag sat there nodding his antlers.

"I understand," he said. "That's exactly how it is."

Why The Hell Would I Do That?

"And that's not all she told me," said Ellie.

"No?" I said.

"No."

"Go on, then," I said.

"She said you sit watching the window. She said you watch the window like you're looking out of it, but she doesn't think you are."

"Oh, really?"

"Yes, really," said Ellie. "She said she thinks you're watching a reflection."

"Watching a reflection?" I said. "Why the hell would I be watching some girl in a reflection? Why the hell would I do that?"

Ellie looked at me for a moment. "I don't know," she said, "maybe you're just watching the traffic."

Another Week in Rio

She lay on a towel in the sun, rested back on her elbows. The sand felt hot enough to burn your skin. She opened her eyes and watched him coming out of the sea. She watched him and the way, after a few steps, he made a mouth and started running on tiptoes. She did not smile. When he sat down some sand flicked up onto her thigh. It stuck in the sun cream.

"There are loads of girls with them on," he said, smiling. "I don't know why you're so bothered about it."

"I'm not bothered about it," she said. "I'm just not wearing it."

"But they're all wearing them."

"Of course they are. We're on Copacabana beach."

"Exactly my point," he said with a little laugh. He put his sunglasses on and sat holding his knees. "I mean, look at her, Arbuckle, there."

She didn't say anything.

"Look at her. And look at you."

"She's tanned and probably Brazilian," she said. "I'm from Stockport."

He shifted on his towel. "What does that matter?"

"Anyway, you're wrong," she said. "She's natural and lovely, and she doesn't care what you think."

"She should," he said. "Size of her."

She looked off, away from him. "That's just not nice," she said.

He laughed. "It's not hurting her."

"Anyway," she said, "I'm not wearing it."

He leaned over to her. "Come on," he said, "I bought it for you. It cost me twenty reals."

"Twenty reals is about four pounds," she said. "Anyway, I'm not."

"Come on. It was the skimpiest one they had." He poked her in the side and laughed. "I know you want to really."

"No. You don't," she said. She looked off at the beach as it curled away from her. The other side of the beach looked very far away.

"I don't know why you bought it anyway," she said.
"We have this convention of giving things to people we like," he said. "We call these things, presents." He winked at her and put his hand on her hip. "Do you need lotioning up yet?"

Lotioning up. She cringed.

"I'm fine," she said. "Anyway, you didn't buy it for me, you bought it for you."

"That's not fair," he said. "It's true, but it's not fair."

He squeezed sun cream into his hand and began rubbing it into her skin, high on her thigh.

"Careful," she said. "There are people around."

"These are the vulnerable areas," he said. "I have to get them."

She lay back on her towel. They had another week yet. Another week in Rio.

She looked at the cloudless sky. It was a funny sepia colour through her sunglasses. She felt him lean across her and start working her other thigh. Then he started on her stomach.

She kept her eyes closed beneath her sunglasses.

Softly Sleeps the Calm

"Give me another shot of that," he said.

I gave him a shot.

"Oh, that's right," he said. "That's the stuff."

The pretty girl next to him said something I didn't hear.

"No," said the man. "You've had enough."

"Come on," said the girl.

"You're done," said the man.

I watched the girl for a while. The old feller down the end started up again, but I took no notice of him. The girl was slumped in her chair. Her hair was scruffed up now and she was sweating. Every so often her eyes would close and then she would jump, just a little start, like something had scared her. I was drinking shots with the man and watching the girl. Her skirt was scrunched up underneath her.

The old feller came over then. He stood there. "I'm a fighter," he said. He was holding his pint glass. "I'm a fighter, but I don't like fighting."

I looked at the other man and he smiled. "Lucky for us then," he said.

A group of people came in. They were types, you know, and they talked to each other as if they were really talking to each other. It took them a while to settle and while they were settling I had a good look at them.

I thought they looked like insects.

"Come on," said the girl waking up. "I want some."

"Here," said the man.
I gave the man a shot and we ignored the girl. She went back to sleep. She sat there sleeping and eventually a little dribble of something ran down her chin.

She was a very pretty girl.

Trust

He dialled again, waited.

- The cell- phone you are calling is switched off.

He walked over to the window and looked through the blinds. He swore.

He paced, dialled. He swore, dialled. He swore loudly.

After he redialled, he waited. Then he threw the phone on the bed.

He pulled up the blind, opened the window and leaned out. There was a close tight air outside. Music from the pub down the road came to him, along with people laughing. Girls laughing, having a good time.

He dialled, waited. He redialled, waited.

He leaned out of the window again and looked. He came back in and pulled down the blind. It clanked against the wall.

He dialled and listened.

- The cell- phone you are calling is switched off.

He went to the CD player, took out the disk, and put it back in its cover. He put in another disk and hit the play button. He fractionally turned down the volume.

Outside someone shouted. He went to the window and looked through the blind. Then he moved the blind and leaned out and looked down the street.

It wasn't her.

Some people, a group of jolly boys and girls having a good time together, passed by in the street and looked up at him. He made as if to look for her and he was looking for her, but he knew she wasn't there. He knew that he looked funny to these people, all serious on a Friday night, with them pleasantly merry and close, all the boys and girls together. They walked past and he heard the girls giggling at him.

He came in and dialled.

Then he dialled again.

He stood and swore.

Then he dialled again.

- The cell-phone you are calling is switched off.

He sat on the window-sill and swung the blind with his knee. Then he picked up the phone.

- The cell-phone you are calling is switched off.

He pressed redial.

- The cell- phone you are calling is switched off.

He swore and dialled again. There was a slight pause and a click, then-

- The cell- phone you are calling is switched off.

He shouted and threw the phone on the bed, and this time as he paced he punched the back of his door. It only made a small dent, but he cut his knuckle.

He sat on the bed. Two minutes went by and he didn't dial at all. He refused to dial. Then it made him angry that he didn't dial because he might have missed her. He dialled quickly.

- The cell- phone you are calling is switched off.

Carson had said, "Yeah, Jonesy's going, Pete, Giles, Damo, they're all going."

"What about Vincent?" he'd said.

"Oh, yeah, Vincent'll be there," Carson said, and looking at him had added, "that prick."

He swore. He got up, walked to the mirror, looked at himself. He walked back to the window.

He looked at the pages of type on his desk. He swore again and his face was hot. The clock said two thirty-five.

People started coming down the road from the clubs. He watched them through the blinds, girls with their arms round boys, boys stopping in the road to kiss girls, people singing, pairing up, having a good time.

- The cell-phone you are-

- The cell-phone...

He dialled and dialled again.

- The cell- phone you are calling is switched off.

"Oh, yeah, Vincent'll be there," Carson had said. "That prick."

He dialled.

Love and Catches 1

When I realised I loved you it was Sunday morning, the time I used to play football. It suddenly hit me that I was in love with you, and the first thing that came to mind was a catch I made in a play-off game years before.

We were in the kitchen cooking breakfast and you had on an old shirt of mine, completely unbuttoned, and a little lacy thong in petrol blue. You were laughing at me because I couldn't concentrate on scrambling the eggs with you walking around like that. We were both laughing and you said I should do something simple like making coffee.

I stood waiting for the kettle to boil and at that precise moment I knew I loved you. It was a hard sudden shock and it made me think of that catch.

No one remembers it now, it was just another catch. I went across the middle, caught the ball for a first down and kept the winning drive going. I took a hell of a shot from their linebacker and as I got up I had mud in my eyes and mouth, and it was one of the truest things I ever felt.

It was the best catch I ever made.

Sometimes You'd Think You Were Goddesses

"Don't worry," said the fat man, "even cowboys get saddle-sore sometimes. And how about those steel workers, ever see them?"

The girl shook her head, but didn't look up.

"Those guys, working twelve, fifteen stories up for years and years and it never bothers them. Then one day someone finds them clinging to a girder, petrified. Scared shitless they're so high up, poor fuckers."

The girl didn't say anything. She rolled the beads of her dress round in her fingers. She kept her eyes on the beads and the way they danced and sparkled in the light.

"It's okay," said the fat man, "you'll be fine. Shit like this happens. Thing to do is to get right back on it, as they say, straight back to it, so it don't get time to fester. You know."

The fat man went over to the girl and sat down next to her on the sofa. He lit a cigarette, sucked it into life and handed it to her. After a pause she took it and swallowed a deep drag. The fat man put his hand on the girl's thigh.

"Okay?" he said.

The girl didn't move or say anything. Smoke drifted up into her face and there was music coming in faintly from the next room.

"I said, *Okay*?"

The girl didn't say a word.

The fat man got up. "You girls," he said, "sometimes you'd think you was goddesses the way you are." He walked over to the door. "Clean this place up," he said. "Then clean yourself up and get out here." The fat man went out of the room then turned and shoved his head back in.

"And tell those other lazy bitches to get out here too."

The girl sat on the sofa and let the fat man's cigarette fall to the floor. She was still twirling the beads of her dress in her hand. She watched the beads and the light they made, gold and silver flashes and sparkles. She watched the lights and as she watched, smoke from the fat man's cigarette drifted up and up into her eyes.

Seventy-Six Trombones

I was at the funeral of a venerable member of the local community.

We had known each other since childhood and they thought we were friends, but in truth I couldn't stand the old sod.

"We would very much like you to be a pall-bearer," they'd said.

"Would you be a pall-bearer for us?" they'd asked.

I said it would be a great honour.

It was all going swimmingly until, as we passed the mourners all lined up holding flowers and handkerchiefs, crying and sobbing, I got a fit of the giggles.

I think they noticed. Some of them at least. But it didn't matter because just then I had a sudden urge, and began to play an imaginary trombone. With my arms as the trombone I blew air through my lips and made a sound like a trombone. "Seventy-Six Trombones" was the tune I played, and I danced and played in the air and tromboned out the tune with my lips.

The other pall-bearers were fantastic. They managed to compensate for my not holding the coffin, and though it was a bit of a scramble, they didn't drop it. They even managed to pop the lid back on before too many people noticed.

The mourners were shocked. Some said it was frightful. But I don't think I've ever played it better.

The End of Something

After lunch they couldn't find anything else to do and Sara decided they would go for a long a walk through the park. It was very hot and they hardly said a thing to each other as they walked, though Sara did say how beautiful it was that the sun was finally out.

Sam didn't say anything. He was done with analysing things.

They went through the woods by the river and coming out into the main field decided to sit on the grass. Sara rested back on her elbows. She closed her eyes and lifted her face to the sun. "It really is hot," she said.

Sam was ripping grass and tossing it into the air.

Sara laughed. "It's a hot exemplary day," she said.

Sam kept quiet. He didn't know what she was talking about. She was always saying something that meant something else and he was sick of it.

"Don't you just love it when it's hot like this?" Sara said.

"Not when you're wearing the wrong shirt," he said.

Sara looked at him and he showed her the areas on his shirt where the sweat was soaking through.

There was a breeze and they drank water and Sara shared out the chocolate she had between them. Then they carried on through the park and went across the big bridge towards town.

They came out by the main traffic lights and a car slowed as it went past them. Sam saw the boys in the car laughing, and he saw the dark haired boy leaning out of the window swearing at him. Sam saw what was happening but he couldn't move quickly enough. The boy squirted him with a huge water-pistol, completely soaking his shirt and shorts. He could see the boys laughing as they drove away.

Sara wanted to laugh. They went on towards the high street and she wanted to laugh, he knew it. She said it didn't matter, that they were just stupid boys and it wouldn't take long to dry, but she wanted to laugh, he could tell.

They found a coffee shop and sat outside, but neither of them said anything for a while. Then Sara began to talk about the weather. She said how great it was to feel the warmth of the sun. She said it made her feel free, that to her it was freedom, unrestricted freedom and release. She laughed and said that summer, for her, was in principle democratic and in character anarchistic. In the best possible sense of course.

Sam didn't say anything. Not a thing. He kept looking at Sara out of the corner of his eye, but he didn't say a word.

Under the hot sun his clothes were gradually drying.

Joe Theisman's Leg

That was the day the bailiffs came.

It was the first time and I was in the kitchen. I had an old scourer in my hand and it made me sick to look at it. Someone had washed up with it earlier and now I was running hot water into the basin, piling the washed dishes back in to soak them. I had the scourer in my hand, looking at all the scum and crud on it. Then the doorbell went and a knock at the door.

From outside, if you looked through the letterbox you could see right across the front room into the kitchen, and a second before the letterbox went, I took one step back against the wall. After a while they stopped looking through the letterbox and I managed to get up to my room.

The pressure was too much. I'd tried to cry it all out, but I couldn't cry. Nothing could release it. I sat staring at the wall, staring at nothing for twenty minutes. Then two things happened. First, the woman next-door began sex-moaning in her bedroom, proper loud grunts and moans. I put my ear to the wall and could hear it clearly. Then my computer chimed an email receipt. I had my ear tight against the wall. The bed was squeaking and my neighbour was making a high-pitched barking sound. There was the sound of skin being slapped and sex-swearing.

And I couldn't cry.

I got away from the wall and clicked on the email. It was from Pete Sligo. In the subject box it said, Joe Theisman's Leg, and below Sligo had typed, Remember this?

I clicked the link and this poor quality video came up, with the date 18th November 1985. And there's Redskins quarterback Joe Theisman handing off – I'd forgotten how it went – and the running back flips the ball to Theisman on a flea-flicker, and then Theisman gets swallowed up as the pocket collapses. For a moment it's nothing, just a sack for a loss. Then you see Lawrence Taylor jump up and gesture frantically to the sideline. He holds his head in his hands as though he's seen something terrible.

The commentators don't know what it is, but they know it's something. They're waiting for the replay. Then it comes. Reverse angle, slow motion, as Theisman steps up and Taylor flies at him, pulling him down and back, and there it is, Theisman's right leg beginning to fracture and break underneath him, bending sideways at the shin at impossible angles.

Through the wall I hear my neighbour finishing up with some crazy high-pitched squealing, and I'm crying now. I'm crying and it won't stop. Watching Joe Theisman's leg break again and again, over and over, and crying and crying.

And downstairs, in another time, someone shouts through the letterbox.

Sunlight on the Side of a House

It wasn't home anymore.

She drove past once without looking. She wanted to drive on and forget about it, but she turned back and saw his van there.

She was collecting stuff that was all. There was nothing else. And she wasn't angry because it was nothing to her now.

She parked and instead of letting herself in she rang the bell. He opened the door. He looked sad and terrible, but it was nothing to her. She said, "All right," looking straight at him without a smile. She went in and picked up her post.

He had all these things to say, she could see it in his eyes, things he had practised saying. Oh, such contrition, such love. She knew it. Such pain. But it didn't touch her, not now.

"How are you?" he said. It came out in a little squeak.

"Very well," she said.

He stood by the door as she began collecting things together, separating her stuff from his. She could see him hovering outside, but it didn't concern her. Nothing about the situation concerned her anymore.

After a minute or two he came in and stood by the fridge. He watched her moving things and every sound she made was very loud.

"I have feelings too," he said then. "You're not the only one that's hurt."

She looked at him. She had a frying pan in her hand and it made a loud clanging sound as she put it down.

"You have feelings?" she said. She started opening cupboards.
"Where are they then? I can't seem to find them. Are they in here?" She opened the oven and the fridge. "What about here?" She got on her knees and looked under the sink. "Where could they be, your feelings?" She opened drawers. "They must be here somewhere if you say you have them."

She turned to him, but he wasn't there. She listened for a moment and then took her things to the car.

As she shut the car door, she hesitated. There was a sudden weight to the moment as the sun cut through the cloud. It was quiet and she watched how the sunlight came across the drive and rested so softly on the side of the house. It was like a caress. She had never noticed it before and she watched it come.

She watched it and tried to empty it of meaning. It had been a long time since she had seen anything like it.

I Should Have Said Something

On Wednesday she pushes hair back from her face and says, "I'm thinking of leaving you, John."

I'm taking off my socks and have a sock in my hand. I'm stunned and ask why.

"It's complicated," she says. "It's me, not you." She looks at her palms. "I've changed. I've changed in more ways than I thought possible. It's a transformation."

On Friday when I return she is calm. "John," she says, "I've been thinking about what I said and I'm sorry. I am so sorry, John."

I let out a hard sigh of relief, and smile as my eyes well up. "It's okay," I say. "Everything's going to be all right."

For a second she just stands there with this horrified look on her face.

"No," she says.

"Yes," I say. "It's not your fault. You're not wrong to feel like this." I move to put my arms around her. "We can work it out. Just like we always do."

She steps away from me in absolute horror.

"No, no, no," she says, her hands up as if fending me off. "I'm sorry for not being honest with you. I'm sorry I didn't tell you about Harris. I should have told you. I should have said something."

"I'm in love with him, John."

The Mentor

He was a big kid, like you could see the power in him and when he looked you in the eye, even if he was trying to be nice, you could see the emptiness there.

"I just loved to fight," he said. "I love it."

"How do you love it?" The mentor shook his head. "I don't understand."

"The buzz of it, I don't know. It's a buzz."

The kid spoke in an accent that was south London with a hint of Jamaican.

"I just love fighting," he said. "You know. You're black."

The mentor looked at the kid. "What does that mean, I'm black?"

The kid laughed awkwardly. "Well, you are."

"Is this a problem for you?"

"No."

"Why did you make it an issue then?"

"I didn't make it an issue."

"What then?"

"You know how it is to fight."

"Pardon me?"

The kid coughed and moved in his seat. "You know how it is to fight," he said. "Don't pretend like you don't."

"I've never had a fight in my life," the mentor said.
The kid laughed.

"I've never had a fight in my life," the mentor said.

The kid looked him in the eye. He went to say something and stopped.

"That's what I'm trying to show you," said the mentor. "There are different stories. Not everyone's had the life you've had. Not everyone has to. You don't have to."

"I can't believe you never had a fight," the kid said.

"It's true. I've never allowed violence to get the better of me."

"What if you had to?"

"I wouldn't have to. I wouldn't allow the situation to arise."

"You can't control things."

"No, but you can control your own actions."

The kid shook his head. "But what if you had to?" he said. "How do you know you could?"

The mentor sighed and went over to the window. "I don't know," he said, moving the blind. "But if I absolutely had to, I would find a way."

"But how do you know?" said the kid.

Something Not So New

All night they'd argued. It started even before they were drunk, and now they were walking home still arguing, and their heads were buzzing because the music was loud in the club.

They were talking in circles. And they were now so drunk and so far from the original argument that neither of them knew what the hell they were arguing about. He knew *she* was drunk because when he said something cutting, which he did easily now, she would start her sentences by saying, "Yes, but no." He knew *he* was drunk because he *was* drunk, though in himself he thought he was pretty sober.

They came to the top of her road and usually it was the best part of walking home with her because he could see her house in the distance. Now, though, as he looked at her bedroom window, it made him feel steely and outside himself and sick.

She turned into her road, but he stopped and right at that moment they sobered up because they both knew this was something different for them, and that something was changed. He stood away from her, not looking at her, and she said his name then, in a question.

The taxis were noisy going by, taking drunk people back from the clubs.

He couldn't move. He could see the cars in the windows of the car showroom across the road. They were flawless, so perfect he couldn't imagine anyone actually driving them. He felt a long way off then and when she spoke to him, his name, all he could say was, "I don't know," and inside everything felt ridiculous.

That was how they were, and the taxis would go past and then there were no taxis and the road was quiet.

She said, "It's up to you." She was looking at him. Her shoulders were down, with her head tilted slightly to the side. Then she turned towards her house. She took five steps, but he didn't move and she stopped. She said, "I can't do any more. What do you want me to do?"

He couldn't say anything. The cars were so shiny. The lights in the showroom were bright and the cars looked pure and clear.

"It's up to you," she said, and this time when she walked she didn't stop walking.

He thought about it all as he stood there and it was ridiculous. There was nothing around and there were no cars and no other sounds. Just the night and the traffic lights changing. Then a car came along. It was old and he watched as it crawled past him. It wasn't new and sharp like the showroom cars. That he could see clearly.

Frozen Peas

Then there was the rain, but she wasn't thinking about that. As she put down her coffee the bracelet on her wrist made a clinking sound. She went into the hall, picked up the post. She did not look at her face in the mirror. Out of the corner of her eye she was drawn to the mirror, was aware of it, and saw a moment of shade there. Looking, but not looking; or was it not looking, but looking?

She put the post on the kitchen table, unopened. The kitchen was quiet. She finished her coffee, wrapped the remainder of the croissant in a piece of kitchen roll and put it in the fridge. She ate two grapes and did not think about her face.

She bit her nails and then did things in the kitchen. She did things that needed doing like wiping down clean surfaces and refolding dishcloths.

The rain came harder outside. She could hear it on the patio. Resting her hands on the sink she watched the hard pounding rain on the garden.

The hot tap was running. It was piping out very hot water and the steam came up out of the sink. She caught her reflection in the kitchen window as she watched the steam. She looked at her face. She looked at the shadows on her face.

She stopped the hot water and went to the freezer. Some ice fragments fell from the freezer shelves as she searched. The ice would melt and leave little puddles, but she didn't care. She sat at the table with the bag of frozen peas in front of her. It was a solid frozen lump, and she thumped it down and it was hard and cold on her hand. She thumped the frozen peas to break them up. The sound of her thumping the peas was loud in the kitchen and she was suddenly very aware of it.

The skin beneath her eye pulsed. She touched her fingers to it.

She had seen it in films. It wasn't peas in films, but real ice. They always had just the right ice that didn't need breaking up, in films.

She picked up the bag and held it to her eye, and took it away at once. After a moment she held it to her eye again. It cooled her eye, but her hand was cold. She needed a tea-towel.

She sat there with the bag to her eye. The rain had eased off. She thought about the tea-towel.

She had no idea what she would do after.

Forget Me, Joe

The rosebush overhangs the path. Its thin branches stretch out for me in the wind. As I move to avoid them, the wind gets up and rose thorns scratch my face.

Lizette was coming out of the bathroom with just her bra on. She looked at me and smiled. She was late again.

"You'll never forget me, Joe," she said. "Whatever happens, you'll never forget me."

I didn't say anything. I was on the stairs, sitting on the second to top stair, watching Lizette get dressed. She put her knickers on and stepped into some black tights. When they were just above her knees she stopped and smiled at me.

I step back from the path. The thorns have grazed my cheek and there's a blood smudge on my fingers. I'm irritated and try to bend the stem back out the way, but the wind gets up again and this time I end up with thorns in my fingers and scratches on my arm.

Lizette came home and lifted the skirt of her suit as she went into the bathroom. I heard her underwear coming down and the sound of her peeing. I sat on the bed and watched her through the open door.

"Don't go anywhere," she said.

I watched her tear paper and wipe herself. She flushed the toilet and came into the bedroom.

"Dinner's on," I said.

Lizette stood in front of me with the skirt up around her waist. The black tights were there again, down around her knees, and I leaned forward and kissed her. Then she let go of the skirt and I was in the dark.

"You'll never forget me, Joe," she said.
I'm sucking where thorns have drawn blood on my hand.
There are faint tracks of blood on my arm.
Behind me on the lawn my child plays with worms and mud and ladybirds.
And she knows nothing of nothing yet.
In my head, Lizette undresses, says, "Forget me, Joe. Forget me."

The Juggler

An old man opened the door and brought the cold in. I went over to the window seat and as I sat down my knee knocked against the metal rail underneath. My coffee spilled on the bench.

The old man said, "Goodness, what a day."

The barista, the one with the red hair tucked up in a black hair-band, agreed smiling.

I used napkins to mop up the coffee, and watched a juggler juggling outside. He was juggling three pins and there were thirty or so school kids around him. The kids were on a field trip or something, wrapped up in their coats, standing with their clipboards and pens as though the juggler might say something important.

The other people in the square, walking through with hard-set faces, none of them looked at the juggler. But the kids looked at him. I watched them watching him – how they smiled and laughed as the juggler flipped the yellow pin under his leg and now behind his back.

My phone lit up. Jen was calling again. The phone was on silent and I watched the symbol on the display shake until it stopped shaking.

1 Missed Call, it said on the display.

The juggler now had four pins going. The kids were all around him, and there was a pigeon sat on a nearby statue.

My phone lit up, a text. I thought it was Jen, but it was Lucy. I read the message. Then I read her previous message and the one before that.

I watched the juggler outside, juggling without a break, captivating the kids, the kids consumed by his juggling.

Another text. Jen was worried. Ring me asap, it said.

The juggler threw a high pin, caught it behind his back, and took a bow. The school kids clapped and cheered. They were having fun being away from school. Then a tall black girl stepped forward to put some change in the juggler's hat on the ground. The other kids looked for change and put it in the hat too.

The juggler picked up four coloured balls and began again.

A text came through, Lucy. You won't answer, it said, but this isn't going away.

I finished my coffee and put the mopped-up coffee napkins in the cup.

The juggler continued in the square. Most of the school kids had gone now, but there'd be more along in due course.

Slag Monkey

The beautiful model in the white bikini loomed above us all.

The station guard was doing a very poor job of explaining why no trains were running from Charing Cross and why, if we wanted to catch a train at all, we would have to go to Victoria. Irate, male commuters were gathering, demanding information. The guard was being harangued on all sides by testosterone and I stepped away from it, and looked at the billboard model. She was young and flawless, not a blemish on her anywhere. Her three-foot smile dazzled with its pure good-heartedness.

None of my fellow commuters resembled the model. Not in looks or in essence. They had frowns, hard faces and sadness in their eyes. The model had a perfection you didn't find at a rush-hour train station. She was immaculate and other worldly, standing there in frozen isolation above a station concourse. I thought I felt sorry for her, but in reality I just felt sorry. I was on the way back to my parents. They said I could stay with them while I got things sorted out.

The day outside was thick with heat and standing traffic and people trying to get home. I made the mistake of slowing down as I tried to decide what to do, and was quickly swept along by the throng behind me. I crossed one road, then another and without making a conscious decision to do so, found myself walking to Victoria.

I cut across Trafalgar Square, and coming towards the arches leading to St James's Park noticed, on one of those grand white-stone buildings, someone had scrawled the words 'chuff muppet' in bright red ink.

Chuff muppet. As graffiti on a white-stone building it was horrible, but the words chuff muppet made me smile. I walked on, wondering whether my smile condoned the graffiti, then a little further on under a window, more of the

same scrawl. It said 'skunk bunny', and this time it was underlined.
Again I walked on smiling, turning the words over in my head without coming to any firm conclusions. But as I came through the archway, on the wall to my left were two huge words in red ink. I stopped and stared at them.

A young couple, a boy and a girl in their late teens, approached from the opposite direction.

"Are you OK?" the girl asked.

"Yes. Sorry," I said, looking at the words. "I saw this."

The girl looked. "It's just graffiti," she said.

"Just graffiti," I said. "There's more back there. 'Skunk bunny' and 'chuff muppet'. What on earth is 'chuff muppet' anyway?"

The boy laughed and stopped himself, like it was the most inappropriate thing he could do.
"This one's my favourite though," I said.

The girl studied the wall again. "Why?" she said.

"Because it's the perfect description of someone I know."

The three of us stood there a little awkwardly, and then boy and the girl smiled and shrugged and walked on.

The trains were delayed at Victoria. I bought coffee and a dried-up croissant, and tried to read my book, but it was hopeless. Something very definite and profound hovered on the edge of my thoughts, but I didn't know what it was.

Later, on the train, I dozed and thought about names. I thought about the billboard with its young model, and how, very distinctly, the guard had called it Cha-re-an Cross and not Char-ring Cross. At some point I changed my seat and watched things out the window go slowly into the distance instead of rushing by. There was so much and it was all very clear, though I couldn't tell you why.

Duration

That mug of tea steamed and I left it on the table awhile to cool.

She was gone and that was all there was to it.

Three seagulls started up on the railing. I didn't know what they were fussing about. It looked like a ritual, some kind of very intense seagull ritual, that even if I spoke seagull I wouldn't understand. I watched them carry on for some time, until it was done, they were done with it, and they flew off; in various directions, I noticed.

For a while I watched the railing. Just the railing, painted a turquoise blue, and people walking by the railing. Then the man came across followed by the dog.

"Good girl," the man said, pointing to a plastic pot on the ground filled with water. The dog didn't look at the man, but went and drank from the plastic pot. The man sat down and ordered something and I watched him, an old man, and noticed his tatty clothes and that his hair was uncut and greasy, but that his manner was calm and courteous. His dog lapped up the water, then came over and sat by his feet under the table.

I drifted. I watched the various blues of sea and sky and railing.

The old man drained his mug. "Good old girl," he said. He got up from the table and shuffled off, pulling slightly ahead, then waiting for the animal to catch up.

"Going home now," he said to the old dog, and noticing me watching added, "At her own pace."

Fountain

And then there wasn't anything else to say.

He stood looking off across the park and she watched the water in the fountain. They waited for each other to say something that could make a difference, but it was obvious that wasn't going to happen.

"I think I'm going to go," he said.

She was watching the fountain.

He said her name and she looked at him.

"I don't know," she said. She tried very hard to find something to say, and the fountain was there, and the sun was burning her arms.

He stood there. Neither of them spoke. Then he said, "For what it's worth, I still love you."

She was watching the fountain.

"Will you do something for me?" she said. "Will you think very hard about what you just said? Because I have no idea what it means." She looked at him. "If you can tell me what it means, it might make a difference."

He looked off into the park.

"It means I'm still here," he said. "I'm still here when I should have been gone months ago."

"And that means you love me? Maybe it just means you're scared."

"Maybe it does."

The fountain sprayed water in the breeze.

"I love you too, you know."

He wouldn't look at her.

"I'm going to go," he said, and she nodded and he walked away.

She watched him into the distance, until he was just a dot indistinguishable from any other dot. Then she went back to watching the fountain.

Before, she'd just seen a fountain, a unified image. Now, she focused on the water, watching it in the pools first, then, as it came bursting out of the nozzles, she watched it rounding off and arcing. If she watched closely she could see the water separate as it rose to the top of its arc, and the small globules of slowing water would suddenly begin to fall, disappearing into spray.

She thought of fountains and how they were like lives, but she was embarrassed by the thought and she blushed. She tried to think about everything, but it was too much. The sun was burning her arms.

And then it came to her. It was gravity. That's what everything depended on in the end.

She sat and watched the fountain and thought about gravity. She didn't know what to make of it. She thought about gravity and watched the fountain flow in the sun.

Tuesday 11th September 2001

The pigeon was nearly dead. It was resting, not moving. A group of schoolgirls had gathered and stood looking down at it. The shoppers were all busy in the precinct and didn't notice the schoolgirls or the pigeon.

The smaller girl had dark hair tied up at the sides and the back. She had a lot to say and the other girls watched her as she moved. She took a step forward so that her shoes were barely an inch from the pigeon's breast. The pigeon did not move. It seemed so concentrated on its imminent death that it didn't see the shoes. It couldn't see them. The shoes made no difference.

None of the girls was laughing now. They were all watching the shoes and the pigeon. And the pigeon was almost dead.

Then one shoe pushed forward.

The pigeon made a small movement as the shoe kept coming, and moved off to one side. It tried to settle, but the shoe kept coming. The shoe itself was barely moving, but it kept coming.

The pigeon was ready to die, but it could not die now. The schoolgirls followed it, pushed their shoes at it, gently, not spitefully, and kept moving it on whenever it settled.

The pigeon wanted to die. It was ready to die, but it had found its way onto a shopping precinct.

The pigeon's eyes kept closing.

And opening again when it couldn't die.

Love and Catches 2

You are the best catch I ever made.

It was the Southern Conference Championship game and with a minute twenty to go I ran a sideline fade and caught a badly thrown ball between their American linebacker and a Great Britain safety. They broke my shoulder, but it put us in field goal range. They were swearing at me trying to get me in the ambulance, but I sat on the sideline and watched that kick go over.

Watching you in the bath, watching the way your hair is so much darker when it's wet and the way you stand up, let the water run down your body between your breasts and legs and off your hips; and how you stand there soaking wet, smiling and biting your lip because you know I'm there.

You are the best catch I ever made.

Frank Foley lives with his family in Whitstable.
He has a B.A. in English literature from the University of
Wales, Cardiff, and an M.A. in English literature from the
University of Kent.

This is his first published collection.

www.frankfoley.co.uk

Printed in Great Britain
by Amazon